THOMAS & FRIENDS™

The Giant Magnet

BRK 03

D0773931

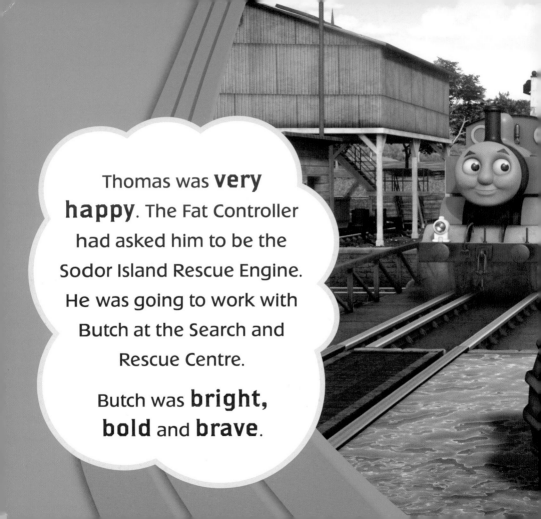

Thomas was **very happy**. The Fat Controller had asked him to be the Sodor Island Rescue Engine. He was going to work with Butch at the Search and Rescue Centre.

Butch was **bright, bold** and **brave**.

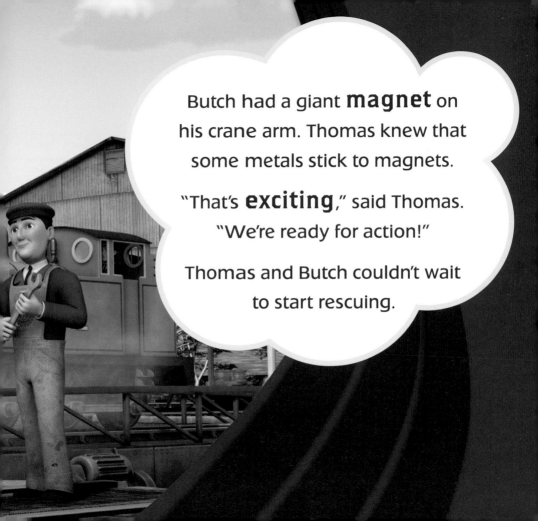

Butch had a giant **magnet** on his crane arm. Thomas knew that some metals stick to magnets.

"That's **exciting**," said Thomas. "We're ready for action!"

Thomas and Butch couldn't wait to start rescuing.

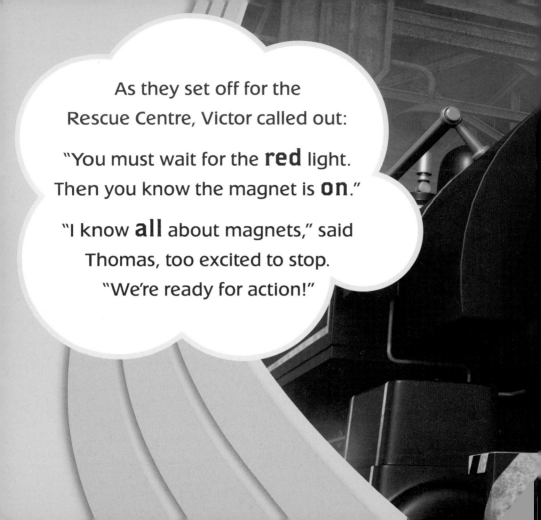

As they set off for the
Rescue Centre, Victor called out:

"You must wait for the **red** light.
Then you know the magnet is **on**."

"I know **all** about magnets," said
Thomas, too excited to stop.
"We're ready for action!"

At the Search and Rescue Centre, an emergency call had just come in. Farmer McColl needed some metal poles. His sheep shelter had blown down!

"This will be **easy**," boasted Thomas, as Butch lowered his magnet over the poles.

But the magnet wouldn't
pick them up.

"Didn't Victor say my red light
should be on?" asked Butch. But
Thomas told him not to worry.

Butch lowered the magnet
further. Then there was trouble.
The big magnet **bashed**
the poles and …

SPLASH!
They rolled into the sea,
right next to Captain!

"Sorry, Captain!" called out Butch.

"We can pick up more poles from
the yard," said Thomas.

But just then **another**
emergency call came in. Rosie's
wheel had cracked! She needed
a new one.

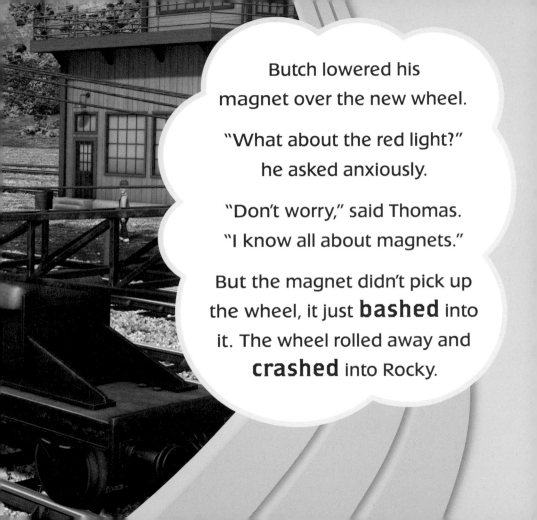

Butch lowered his magnet over the new wheel.

"What about the red light?" he asked anxiously.

"Don't worry," said Thomas. "I know all about magnets."

But the magnet didn't pick up the wheel, it just **bashed** into it. The wheel rolled away and **crashed** into Rocky.

"There's something wrong with my magnet," said Butch.

"I'm metal," said Thomas. "Let's see if it sticks to me!"

So Butch drove up next to Thomas. Suddenly the red light flicked on.

Butch swung his magnet and it stuck tight to Thomas! **CLUNK!**

Butch **pulled** and **pulled** but he couldn't get the magnet off!

"What a silly engine I am," sighed Thomas. "I thought I knew all about magnets, so I didn't listen to Victor. We must go and ask him what to do."

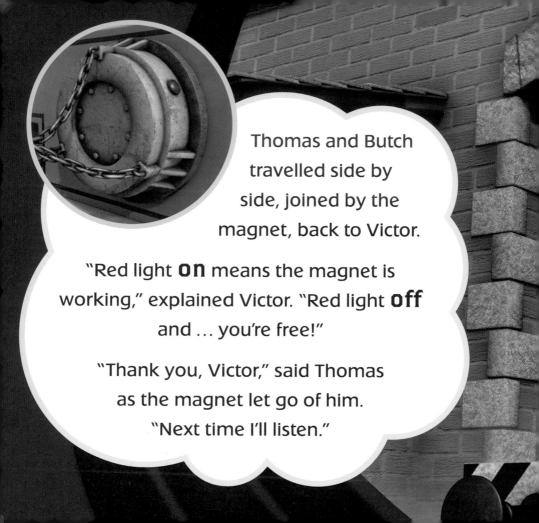

Thomas and Butch travelled side by side, joined by the magnet, back to Victor.

"Red light **on** means the magnet is working," explained Victor. "Red light **off** and … you're free!"

"Thank you, Victor," said Thomas as the magnet let go of him. "Next time I'll listen."

With the help of the magnet, Butch and Thomas delivered the metal poles to Farmer McColl and the new wheel to Rosie.

Everyone thought the giant magnet was **marvellous!**

"Red light on!" cried Thomas.

"Ready for action!" replied Butch.

PEEP! PEEP!

The End